Tweety
AND THE PIG

Written and illustrated by Kezia Olivia Holston

WestBow Press books may be ordered through booksellers or by contacting:

WestBow Press
A Division of Thomas Nelson & Zondervan
1663 Liberty Drive
Bloomington, IN 47403
www.westbowpress.com
1 (866) 928-1240

ISBN: 978-1-4908-6674-1 (sc)
ISBN: 978-1-4908-6675-8 (e)

Library of Congress Control Number: 2015901073

Printed in the United States of America.

WestBow Press rev. date: 02/04/2015

WESTBOW
PRESS
A DIVISION OF THOMAS NELSON
& ZONDERVAN

For

Mama and Daddy

You were always there.

Inspired by a true story,
<u>Tweety and The Pig</u>

is a story about a little girl's faith and determination to work on her father's farm with her big brothers. She is constantly told "No" by her father, until something happens with a pig that changes everything. This one day encounter on the farm marks the beginning of Tweety's talent being discovered, which eventually leads her to the Olympic games later on in life.

One day on a farm, in a small town called Jakin, GA, a baby girl was born to the parents of Papa Daniels and Ma Vera. Papa Daniels and Ma Vera had eight children. Their names were Edith, Thelma, Buddy, Robert, Marjorie, Junior, Marian, and Arthur. The ninth child was born on July 31, 1937. They named her Isabelle Frances Mae Daniels. Her brothers and sisters gave her the nickname "TWEETY", because she sound like a bird when she cried. "Tweet, tweet, tweet," cried Tweety all day long.

Tweety grew up on a big farm. Everyday Tweety's brothers would help Papa Daniels on the farm and Tweety's sisters would help Ma Vera in the house.

Tweety wanted so badly to help on the farm too, but Papa Daniels would say, "No, No, Tweety. You are too little. Wait until you get big."

Papa Daniels was afraid she would get hurt, so Tweety spent many sad days sitting on the steps by herself, watching her brothers work on the farm.

Tweety didn't understand why her daddy would not let her work on the farm too. Tweety knew she could help with some things on the farm. She had to be big like her brothers, but with every day that passed by, it seemed like she was still little and she would never get a chance to work on the farm.

Tweety was a very quiet child and she said her prayers every night. But one night, Tweety didn't say anything. She just cried. God heard her cry and felt the sadness and loneliness in her heart. Tweety didn't have to say a word. God knew all about it.

One day, Tweety was sitting on the steps, as usual, watching her brothers work on the farm. All of a sudden, one of the pigs escaped from the pig pin and ran into Ma Vera's garden.

The pig was stepping all over the collard greens, turnips, tomatoes, and green peppers that Ma Vera had planted.

"Oh No! Look!" shouted Papa Daniels as he pointed to the garden. "One of the pigs done got out again!" Papa Daniels had to think fast before the pig destroyed all the vegetables in the garden.

Tweety's brothers heard Papa Daniels and rushed over to see what was wrong.

This time, Tweety, got up and ran to the garden to see what was going on, but she stood behind the fence and watched so she would not get into trouble.

Papa Daniels was too old to chase the pig so he asked his sons for help. "Ok, boys. Here is the plan. I'm going to send you into the garden one at a time to catch the pig. Buddy, you're first. Buddy was the oldest son and he just knew he could catch the pig. He had dreams of joining the army, so he saluted his brothers, made an about face, and said, "Step back brothers. I can do this."

Papa Daniels opened the fence and Buddy took off chasing the pig. Buddy ran and ran, but Buddy was too slow and taking too long.

Buddy ran out of breath, gave up, and walked out of the garden. Buddy could not catch the pig.

While still watching behind the fence, Tweety says, "Daddy, Daddy, Let me in! I can catch the Pig!" Papa Daniels said, "No, No, Tweety. You are too little. Wait until you get big."

The pig was still running loose in the garden. So Papa Daniels sent Robert inside the garden to catch the pig. "I may not be the oldest son, but I'm the smartest. I have a plan," Robert said. Robert had dreams of joining the army too, so he designed a battle plan to capture the pig. Robert marched to the fence and said," Step back everybody and watch me put my plan into action."

Papa Daniels opened the fence and off Robert ran as fast as he could, chasing the pig. Robert had a master plan to catch the pig but the pig turned left and made a quick right. This was surely not in Robert's plan.

Robert tripped on his feet and fell to the ground and he too could not catch the pig.

While still watching behind the fence, Tweety says, "Daddy, Daddy, Let me in! I can catch the Pig!" Papa Daniels said, "No, No, Tweety. You are too little. Wait until you get big."

The pig was still in the garden and Papa Daniels turned to his third son Junior. Junior dreamed of becoming a preacher and a teacher, so he figured that if he caught this pig, he could teach the pig a lesson, including his brothers.

So he put on his church shoes and ran inside the garden to catch the pig. Junior's church shoes were nice and shiny but they slowed him down.

Junior did not want to get his church shoes dirty so he gave up and tip-toed out of the garden. Junior too, could not catch the pig.

While still watching behind the fence, Tweety says, "Daddy, Daddy, Let me in! I can catch the Pig!" Papa Daniels said, "No, No, Tweety. You are too little. Wait until you get big."

The pig was still in the garden and the sun was beginning to set. Papa Daniel's hopes were fading fast, but he had one more son left. His name was Arthur. Now Papa Daniels just knew that Arthur would catch that old pig. After all, Arthur knew more about farming than any of his brothers. All the children in Jakin, GA loved Arthur, and Arthur had a unique understanding with all of the animals on the farm.

Arthur saw the distressed look in Papa Daniels eyes. "I'm going to give it my best shot Daddy and I'll try to catch the pig, "Arthur said, "but I can't make any promises." With the last bit of hope in his eyes, Papa Daniels said, "Ok, son. If you don't catch the pig, I'll still love you. I love all my children." See Papa Daniels knew that one day Arthur would take over his farmland and be in charge of all the animals on the farm.

So Papa Daniels opened the fence and off Arthur ran trying to catch the pig. The pig slowed down to trick Arthur into catching him, but Nope!! The pig sped up, zipped passed Arthur and hid behind the carrots in the garden. Arthur too, could not catch the pig.

Poor Papa Daniels. It seemed like all hope was lost. It was getting darker outside. Papa Daniels had four sons and none of them could catch that pig.

Tweety ran to her father and tugged on his shirt and said, "Daddy, Daddy, Pleeease! Let Me In! I CAN CATCH THE PIG!"

Papa Daniels looked down at Tweety and saw the determination in her eyes. "Ok Tweety. I'll let you in the garden to catch the pig." Papa Daniels didn't think Tweety would catch the pig. After all, Tweety was the baby of the family and she was a girl.

Papa Daniels opened the fence and Tweety took off chasing the pig. Tweety ran and ran and ran. The faster the pig ran, the faster Tweety ran.

The pig made a left and Tweey was right behind it. The pig made a right and Tweety made a right with it.

Papa Daniels eyes popped wide open with surprised. "RUN TWEETY RUN!! Papa Daniels shouted. Robert, Buddy, Junior and Arthur all rushed over to see what Papa Daniels was shouting about.

To her brothers' surprise, they saw Tweety in the garden running after the pig, and Tweety was right on its tail. "GO TWEETY GO!!!!" the brothers shouted waving their hands in the air. "Look at that girl run," shouted Papa Daniels in amazement.

Tweety ran and ran. She ran so fast that she ran right pass the pig! The pig got tired.
It stopped in its tracks and laid down in the garden to catch its breath.

Tweety picked the pig up and ran to her father with a great big smile and said," Daddy, Daddy!!! Look. I caught the Pig!!!!

Papa Daniels couldn't believe his eyes.

Papa Daniels went inside the house and told Ma Vera what he had seen. "Vera. Our baby girl can run and she is fast as lightnin!"

From that day on Papa Daniels let Tweety work on the farm just a little bit, but she mostly "ran" errands for their family. She ran and ran and ran her way to a Bronze Medal in the Olympic Games of Melbourne, Australia in 1956.

The Real Tweety

The Real Tweety Again

The Real Tweety
Winning

Isabelle Daniels Holston
"Tweety"

Born to the parents of Fred and Vera Daniels, Isabelle Daniels Holston became active in sports at an early age and throughout high school. Isabelle's dream was to compete in the Olympic Games. Before graduating from Carver High School in Jakin, Georgia, Isabelle competed in several track events in Blakely, Albany, Fort Valley, Georgia and Tuskegee, Alabama.

With sacrifice, determination and diligence Isabelle was able to earn a track scholarship to **Tennessee State University** in Nashville, TN with **Coach Edward Temple** as her track coach. There she won several national and international awards including a Bronze medal in the 4x100 meter relay during the 1956 Olympic Games in Melbourne, Australia. She won awards at the 1955 Pan American Games in Mexico City, Mexico. She won awards at the 1959 Pan American Games in Chicago, Illinois and the Goodwill Tours where she ran in Moscow, Russia; Budapest, Hungary; Warsaw, Poland and Athens, Greece. She made all American from 1955-1959 in track and field. She was the first Tigerbelle in history to qualify and win 4th place in the 100 meters finals of the 1956 Olympics. She held records in the 60 meters, 50 yard dash, 100 meters, 100 yard dash, and the 220 yard dash.

She ran alongside her other teammates which included Olympic medal winners, **Wilma Rudolph**, **Barbara Jones**, **Martha Hudson**, **Margaret Matthews**, **Mae Faggs**, **Lucinda Williams**, **Shirley Crowder and a host of other legendary Tennessee State University Tigerbelles**.

As a Physical Education teacher and Girls' Track coach in Dekalb County, Isabelle made outstanding accomplishments as a coach for 37 years. Her track team won **seven county titles**, **ten regional titles**, and **four state titles** during her coaching career.

In 1982-1983, Isabelle was named Coach of the Year by the Georgia Athletic Coach's Association. She was also awarded Region III National Coach of the Year by the National

High School Athletic Coaches Association in 1983, 1985, and 1990. In 1992, she was honored as the All-Star Role-Model during a Georgia High School All-Star Basketball game. Within the same year, Isabelle was added to the Coaches Care Honor Roll by the Gatorade Company.

In 1983, Isabelle was inducted into the Tennessee State University Hall of Fame. In 1987, she was inducted into the **Georgia Sports Hall of Fame**. In 2006, she was inducted into the Bob Hayes Hall of Fame. She received the "Key To The City" in her hometown of Jakin, GA, on May 27, 1995. **Isabelle Daniels Holston, along with other Tennessee State University Tigerbelles, carried the Olympic Torch during the 1996 Olympic Games in Atlanta, GA**.

She is currently a member of the Decatur/Dekalb Retired Educators Association and the Georgia Retired Educators Association. At the age of 77, Isabelle still participates in various county, state and national track meets for seniors, where she throws the shot-put, discus, and sometimes competes in the long jump. A great friend and colleague by the name of **Linda Lowery**, is always there to keep Isabelle moving on the track. Isabelle and Linda are both members of the Atlanta Track Club.

Isabelle is married to the Rev. Dr. Sidney R. Holston, Co- Founder of Church Twinning International, Inc., which is a non-profit ecumenical outreach ministry that joins churches in America with churches in Ghana, West Africa, Jamaica, South Africa, Peru and beyond. Rev. Holston has preached about missions work in various churches in the southeastern part of the United States which included churches such as Dexter Avenue King Memorial Baptist church where the late Rev. Dr. Martin Luther King Jr., formerly pastored. He has also preached in Ghana, West Africa at Calvary Methodist Church in Accra, Ghana. The late Dr. Andrew C. Denteh, from Ghana, West Africa, was author and co-founder of Church Twinning International. Isabelle and Sidney have four children, seven grandchildren, and one great grandson. They live in Decatur, GA.

Words from the Author

The book Tweety and The Pig is an attempt to celebrate the legacy of my mother's life and to continue her life as a champion within the minds and hearts of children all over the world. More especially, this book is also an expression of my love for family.

The characters in the story Tweety and the Pig are real people, most of whom have gone to be with the Lord. (**Vera Daniels**, **Fred Daniels Sr.**, **Edith Daniels Ford**, **Edward "Buddy" Daniels**, **Robert Daniels**, **Thelma Daniels**, **Fred Daniels**, **Jr.**, **and Arthur Daniels**) My aunts, Marjorie Daniels Williams, Marian Daniels Walker, and my mom "Tweety" Isabelle Daniels Holston, are the last three siblings living on my mom's side, and I wanted to do something special for them while they are still living.

My father, Rev. Dr. Sidney R. Holston, Co-Founder of Church Twinning International, Inc. has just turned 80 years old. He still speaks when he is invited. He still visits sick people in the hospital. **He still leads our family in Wednesday night devotion and Bible study in our home.** He still mows our lawn, sweeps our driveway, fixes our electrical shortages, repairs our stove and toilets, washes dishes, and takes out the trash among many other things. If we ever lived in a nice, perfect house with no problems, I probably would never get a chance to see how great my father is at the age of 80. **Regardless of what he is doing**, **he always makes himself available to pray for anyone**, **whether they ask for prayer or not**. I couldn't ask for a better dad and I love him very much. Mom, too.

I graduated from Decatur High School and Kennesaw State University with a major in Studio Art. I've held several jobs within the last 15 years mainly in education as a teacher and assistant teacher in private schools, public schools and even correctional facilities where I taught adult literacy. I could never pass the state teacher certification test, but that's OK. God opened doors that allowed me to do what I really wanted to do at that time, and that was helping people of all ages learn to read and write, even though it was only for a short time.

Due to my mental illness, I have limitations that restrict me from engaging in the workforce. Therefore, I just write. Sometimes I write as a form of therapy to temporarily relieve my symptoms of depression, anxiety, paranoia, etc., and sometimes I write because there is just something I need to say, something I need to understand, or somebody I need to talk to when no one is listening.

I was recognized for my artistic gift years ago, but I have recently found a new joy for writing stories that may help children of all ages try to understand each other, try to build better relationships with one another and most importantly try to build a better relationship with God along the way. I'm trying to do that myself. Maybe this is a way for me to teach without being in the classroom. It's like teaching while being taught at the same time, while learning and relearning lessons about life along the way.

I love visual art, but writing makes it a little easier to express myself by using the pen as my paint brush and the words are my colors. I have been told that I have many gifts such as drawing, painting, maybe singing, and writing, but I hope there is one gift that I possess that stands out more than any gift, skill, or talent and that is the gift of love (The love of Jesus Christ). For without the love of Jesus Christ, my gift is not that great and neither am I.

Lord, help me to love others each and every day
And please, teach me, if I say or do
anything that is not of Your way

Printed in the United States
By Bookmasters